The Digging-est Dog

BY **AL PERKINS** ILLUSTRATED BY **ERIC GURNEY**

BEGINNER BOOKS A Division of Random House

Dennis, Douglass, and Derek
with love

http://www.randomhouse.com/

This title was originally cataloged by the Library of Congress as follows:
Perkins, Al.   The digging-est dog.   Illustrated by Eric Gurney.   [New York]
Beginner Books   [1967]   63 p.   col. illus.   24 cm.   I. Gurney, Eric, illus.   II. Title.
PZ8.3.P42Di   j811   67-21920   ISBN: 0-394-80047-8   ISBN: 0-394-90047-2 (lib. bdg.)

Printed in the United States of America
71

I was the saddest dog you could ever see,
Sad because no one wanted me.
The pet shop window was my jail.
The sign behind me said, "For Sale."

3

I was tied to a bare, hard floor of stone.

I could not even dig for a bone.

I was living all of my life alone,

A dog that no one wanted to own.

And then one day, at half-past four,
Sammy Brown came in the door.
Sam took one look at me and cried,
"Why are you tied up here inside?

"I've always wanted a dog like you,
So I'll tell you what I'm going to do.
I'll take you out to the farm with me.
You'll play outdoors where you should be."

I felt as happy as a pup
When Sam paid the man and picked me up.
He rubbed my ears. He scratched my head.
"I think I'll call you Duke," he said.

Sam gave me a collar. He gave me a lead.

We left that shop at tre-men-dous speed.

We went a long way out of town.

We came to the farm of Sammy Brown.

It was the nicest place I'd ever seen,

A pretty white house in a field of green.

And in the shade of the apple tree,
A special dog house just for me!

Next morning, while Sam did his chores,

He let me run and play outdoors.

I'd never played outdoors before.

I'd always lived on that hard floor.

I'd never run on nice soft ground.
Now I barked with joy as I ran around.

Sam looked at me and scratched his head.
"Duke, you need some friends," he said.

He blew his whistle. He blew a blast.
And many dogs came running fast.

I'd never met a dog before.

Now I was meeting six or more.

They walked around and looked at me.

They looked me over carefully.

Then, at last, I heard them say,

"He's one of us. He'll be okay."

One dog, who wasn't very big,

Suddenly began to dig.

The others started digging too.

But that was something I could not do.

I'd never learned to dig in that store.

How could I, on that hard stone floor?

I tried to dig, but, alas, I couldn't.

I wiggled my paws. My paws just wouldn't.

I fell on my ear. I fell on my face.

I fell on myself all over the place.

The others said, "Duke may be big,
But he's no good! He cannot dig."
They stuck their noses in the air.
They walked away. They left me there.

"I'll teach you, Duke," cried Sammy Brown.

"I'll show you how to dig deep down."

He crouched beside me. With his hand

He dug a hole in a pile of sand.

I tried it too. But still I couldn't.

I wiggled my paws. My paws just wouldn't.

I'd never learned to dig in that store.

How could I, on that hard stone floor?

Sammy sighed.

I almost cried.

My eyes and nose were full of dirt.

My paws and claws and elbows hurt.

I had a pain across my back.

I knew I'd never get the knack.

Sam felt sad, and I felt bad.
If only I could make him glad!

We both knew I'd never get it right.
Sam and I couldn't sleep that night.

So, when the sun rose in the sky,
I thought I'd give it one more try.
I wiggled one paw. I saw it could.
I wiggled the other. I saw it would.

I could dig with my paws.
I could dig with my claws.
I felt no pain across my back.
I knew at last I had the knack!

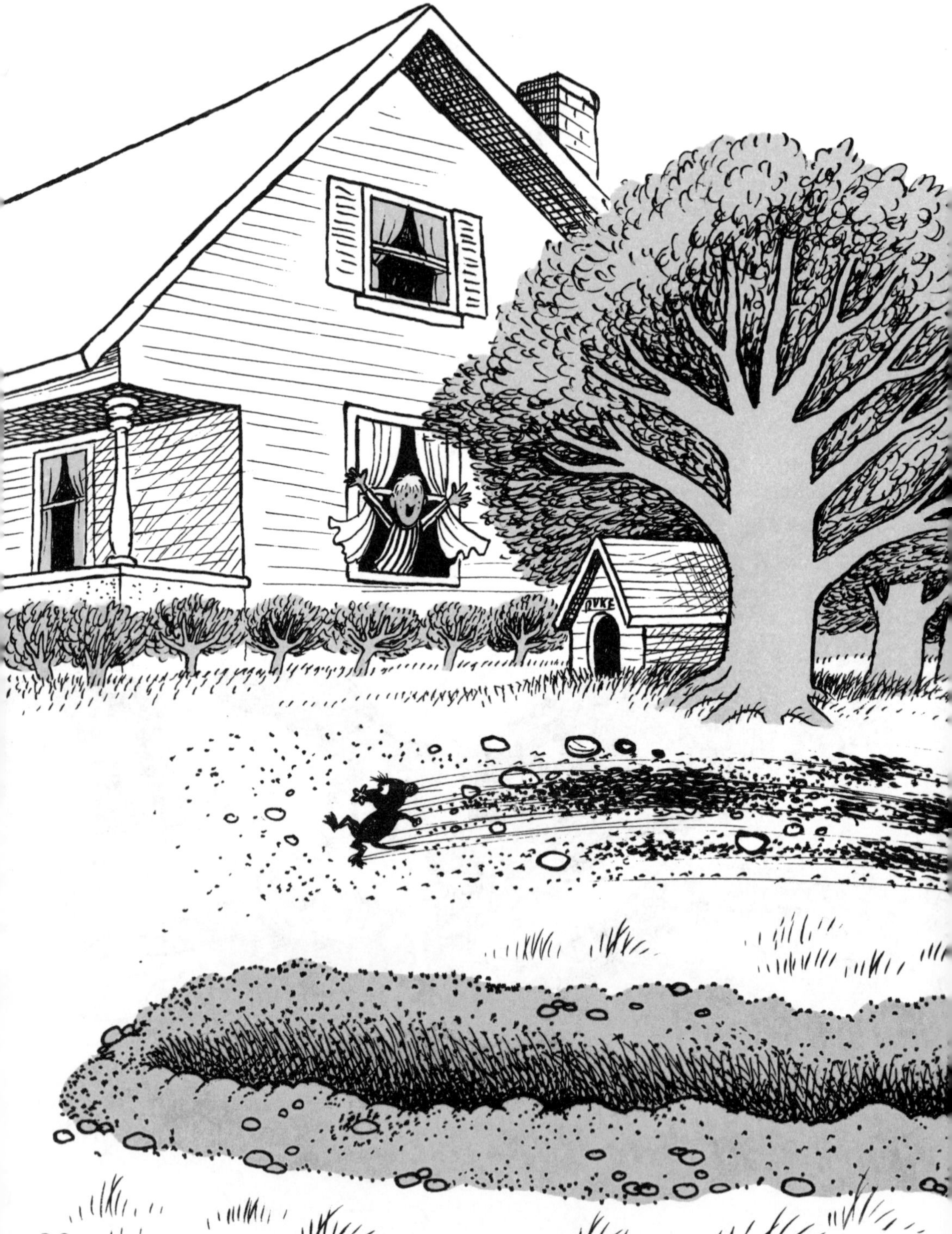
DUKE

Sammy Brown looked out at me.

He saw me digging happily.

"Good for you, Duke!" Sammy cried.

"I knew you'd do it if you tried."

So I dug farther. I dug faster.

I dug and dug to please my master.

I dug up grass. I dug up weeds.
I dug up daisies. I dug up seeds.

I dug up the fence. I dug up the gates.
I dug up the garden of Mrs. Thwaites.

I dug up the rooster. I dug up the hens.
I dug up the sheep and pigs in their pens.

I dug and dug. I couldn't stop.
I dug up the barber in his shop.

I dug up Mister Rodney Thayer,
Sitting in the barber's chair.

I dug my way right through the town.
I dug a lot of buildings down.

I was having so much fun!
I dug up Highway Eighty-One.

I came to a hill. I dug to the top.
But all of a sudden I had to stop.

Right in front of me, looking down,
There stood my master, Sammy Brown!

Sam didn't smile or pat my head.
He only glared at me and said,
"I'm sending you back to that animal store.
They'll tie you to that hard stone floor,
And you'll never, *never* dig any more."

I couldn't run. I couldn't hide.
Dogs came at me from every side.

And then suddenly I knew
There was just one thing for me to do.

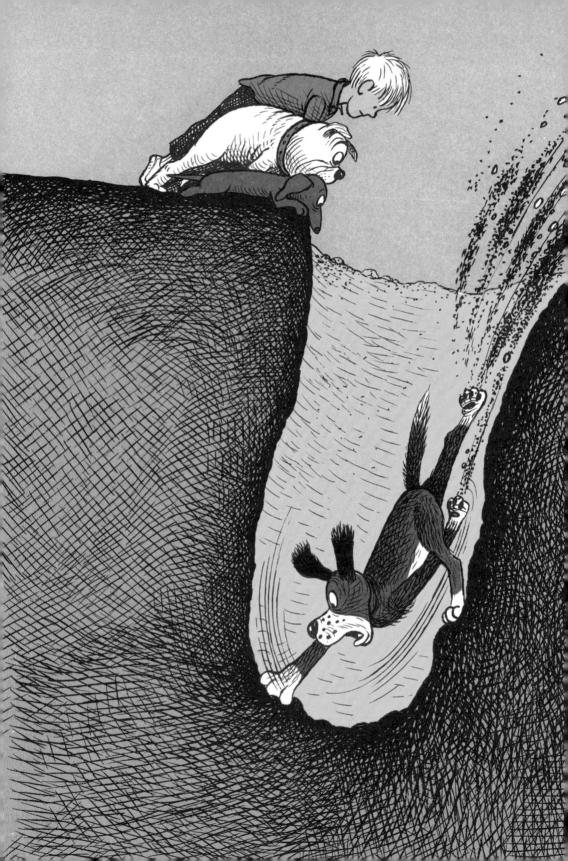

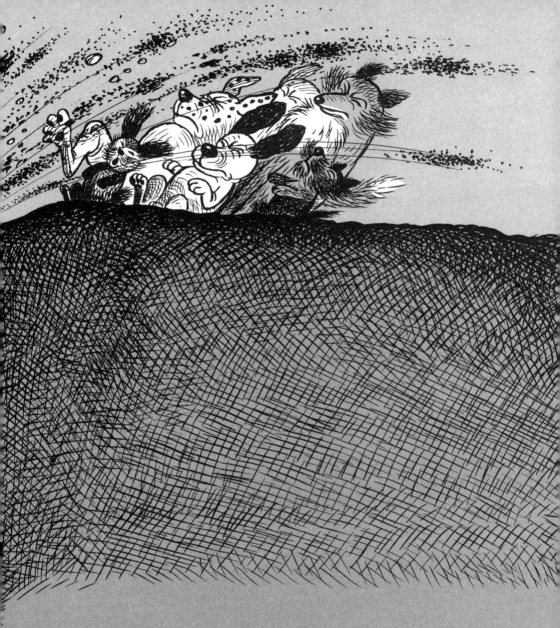

I ran away from Sammy Brown.

I dug a hole that went straight down.

I left him standing up on top.

I dug and dug. I didn't stop.

How deep I dug I could not tell.
But soon I found I'd dug a well!
Mud and water up to my chin!
What a fix I now was in!
I started to sink. I started to yelp.
"Help!" I yelped.
"Help! Help! Help! Help!"

I could hear them way above my head.
I could hear every word they said.
One dog growled, "He wrecked our town.
This serves him right. Just let him drown."

But Sam cried, "Duke! You've been bad.
You've made me sad instead of glad.
But we're not going to let you die.
We'll get you out. At least, we'll try!"

Then at last I heard him shout,

"Maybe we can pull you out!"

Slowly, slowly, down they came,
Each dog part of a long dog chain.
I reached up. I touched a nose.
I felt them lift me by my toes.
Slowly, slowly, bit by bit,
They dragged me up out of the pit.

I thanked the dogs and Sammy Brown.
And then I started back toward town.
I knew I had to dig once more
To fix things up as they were before.

59

That's what I did. I dug back gates.

I dug back the garden of Mrs. Thwaites.

I dug back the roosters and the hens.

I dug back all the pigs and their pens.

I dug all day in the summer sun.
I dug back Highway Eighty-One.
I dug back everything in town—
Everything that I'd knocked down.

Today when I dig—well, I'm careful now.
I'm useful too. Sam lets me plow.
He'll never send me to that store
Or tie me up on a hard stone floor.
My dog friends watch and wonder why
They can't dig as well as I.